D0471909

THE FABULOUS TALE OF FISH & CHIPS

'For my Father, Aaron Becker. May his memory be a blessing'

Helaine Becker

'To my loving parents Orna and Daniel'

Omer Hoffmann

First published in the UK in 2021 by Green Bean Books
c/o Pen & Sword Books Ltd
47 Church Street, Barnsley, South Yorkshire, S70 2AS, England
www.greenbeanbooks.com

Paperback edition: ISBN 978-1-78438-570-5
Harold Grinspoon Foundation edition: ISBN 978-1-78438-574-3

Designed by Saray García Rúa
Edited by Kate Baker, Julie Carpenter & Phoebe Jascourt
Production by Hugh Allan

Printed in China by Printworks Global Ltd, London and Hong Kong
092135K1/B1737/A7

THE FABULOUS TALE OF FISH & CHIPS

Written by Helaine Becker

Illustrated by Omer Hoffmann

Joseph Malin loved fish.
He loved catching fish from the sea.
He loved selling fish in his family's shop.
And, most of all, Joseph loved eating fish.

FURNITURE
MALIN'S FISH
LONDON'S FRESHEST FISH!

His grandmother had taught him how to cook fish to make it extra tasty. She used a special recipe handed down from her grandmother, and her great-grandmother before her.

First, she cut up the fish and coated the fillets in flour.

Then, she dipped the fillets in a bowl of beaten egg.

Next, she quickly dunked them all in a dish of matzoh meal.

Finally, it was time
to fry the fish in hot oil.
It smelled delicious
as it sizzled in the pan!

Joseph's grandma told
him the secret of this
scrumptious recipe.
"It's the crispy crust that
makes the fish so delicious.
And that's why
it still tastes good
when we eat it cold
on the Sabbath."

Eating fish was one thing. That was easy. But selling it was hard.

Although everyone in Joseph's family worked in their shop from dawn 'til dusk, they still made hardly any money. Joseph couldn't even replace his worn-out shoes.

Something had to be done!

One evening, as the smell of his grandma's fried fish wafted through the house, Joseph had a bright idea. "What if we were to sell our fresh fish *after* it's cooked? We could use your secret recipe, Grandma!" he suggested.

"What a marvellous idea!" she said.

The next morning, Joseph's grandma fried enough fish to fill a few trays. He carried the cooked fish to the marketplace.

"Fresh from the ships!

Hot 'n' tasty fried fish!"

Joseph shouted.

At first, just a few curious customers tried Joseph's fish.

But word soon spread and, before long, people were coming from far and wide to try it.

"Yum!" they whooped. "Scrumptious! Galumptious!"

Soon, shiny coins began to pile up in the family till.
“Now we can finally afford to replace your worn-out shoes,”
Joseph’s mother said.

Joseph's shoes were new, but now *he* was worn out. He needed help!

So everyone pitched in. His grandma even bought him a new pushcart to take the fish to the market.

Joseph's family was delighted with his success – but not everyone was happy. Annette, their neighbour, was upset. All her customers were rushing past her vegetable stall and buying Joseph's fried fish instead. What would happen if no one bought her potatoes any more?

Something had to be done!

“That fish does smell
awfully good,”
she muttered
to herself.

Then, she had her
own bright idea.
“If Joseph can sell
fried fish, why can’t I
sell fried potatoes?”

The next morning, Annette cut up some potatoes. She tossed them in hot oil until they were golden-brown and crunchy-crisp, the way *her* own grandmother had taught her.

She made cones out of newspaper, filled them with chips, and started selling them to passers-by.

"Piping hot chips!
Piping hot chips!
They're crisp and delish.
Even better than fish!"
she trilled.

Soon Joseph's customers were scurrying past him to try Annette's fried potatoes.

"Yum!" they whooped. *"Savoury! Flavoury!"*

Joseph fumed. How dare Annette spoil his new business!
What if all his hard work was for nothing?
Something had to be done! He bellowed even more loudly:

"Hot, crispy fried fish!
Hot, crispy fried fish!
Come try my great dish
of hot, crispy fried fish!"

They continued shouting,
not looking where they were going,
until . . .

Disaster!

Chips flipped.

Fish flew.

"Look what you made me do!"
shouted Annette.

"Look what *you* made me do!"
shouted Joseph.

While Joseph and Annette argued, a crowd gathered.
They helped themselves to both the fish *and* chips.

"Scrumptious and galumptious, savoury and flavoury!"

Joseph and Annette eventually stopped arguing and looked at the crowd of delighted people around them. Then, they had a fabulous idea. The next morning, both their voices rang out in perfect harmony:

"Fish 'n' chips!
Chips 'n' fish!
Such a crispy, tasty dish!"

And that's the story of how fish and chips – one of the greatest and most popular dishes of all time – was born.
And what a fantastic pairing it was.

AUTHOR'S NOTE

Joseph Malin really did open up the very first fish and chips shop in London's East End, in 1860. Malin's of Bow, the world's first 'chippy,' operated for more than one hundred years.

Joseph's ancestors had been frying fish for centuries. Spanish Jews fleeing from the Inquisition had first brought their traditional Sabbath dish, *pescado frito* (fried fish), to northern Europe in the late fifteenth century. The dish was typically prepared on Friday afternoons and served cold the next day, the Jewish Sabbath, when cooking was forbidden.

A matzah meal coating kept the fish from tasting oily when served cold. Spanish Jews discovered it also made the fish delicious when hot, and so this recipe became popular wherever they settled.

Did Joseph Malin really get his idea for combining fish with chips from a French woman called Annette? We'll never know, but French and Belgian women are credited with being the first to fry potatoes in hot oil (hence the name 'French fries') and French Huguenots had lived in London's East End since the seventeenth century.

Today, fish and chips is a much-loved dish all over the world and an icon of British cooking. There are more than 10,500 fish and chips shops in the United Kingdom alone, and thousands more around the globe.

FRIED FISH IN THE JEWISH FASHION

The author's own family recipe!

Make with adult supervision.

Ingredients

- 6 meaty white fish fillets – cod, haddock, or halibut
- 2 medium eggs
- 1 cup (250 ml) matzah meal or breadcrumbs
- ¼ tsp. paprika
- salt and pepper to taste
- canola or sunflower oil

Method

1. Pour the matzah meal onto a shallow bowl. Season with salt, pepper, and paprika. Mix thoroughly with your fingers.
2. In a separate bowl, beat the eggs with a fork.
3. Place the fillet in the matzah meal, lightly coating both sides.
4. Swirl the coated fillet in the egg mixture until it is thoroughly moistened. Let the excess drip off.
5. Return the eggy fish to the matzah meal, covering both sides. (Avoid touching with your fingers; the coating will come off the fish.)
6. Repeat for all the remaining fillets. (Do not stack fillets on top of each other.)
7. Put oil in the pan to a depth of ¼ inch. (Don't skimp or your fish will stick and burn!)
8. Heat the oil until it is hot enough for a drop of matzah meal coating to sizzle and dance in the pan. Add the fish to the pan, being careful to keep the fillets separate.
9. Fry the fillets on a medium-high heat until the underside is golden and crisp. Move the fish as little as possible during the cooking.
10. Flip the fish over. Keep frying until the other side is golden brown and the fish is cooked through.
11. Drain the cooked fish on plenty of paper towels or brown paper. Serve at once or refrigerate to eat cold the next day.

Other Green Bean Books

The Magician's Visit
Adapted by Barbara Diamond Goldin
Illustrated by Eva Sánchez Gómez

The Sages of Chelm and the Moon
Written by Shlomo Abas
Illustrated by Omer Hoffmann

Shani's Shoebox
Written and Illustrated by Rinat Hoffer
Translated by Noga Applebaum

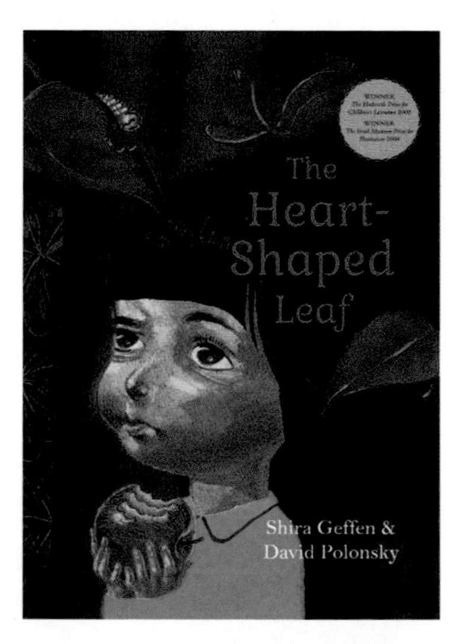

The Heart-Shaped Leaf
Written by Shira Geffen
Illustrated by David Polonsky

Benjy's Blanket
Written by Miguel Gouveia
Illustrated by Raquel Catalina

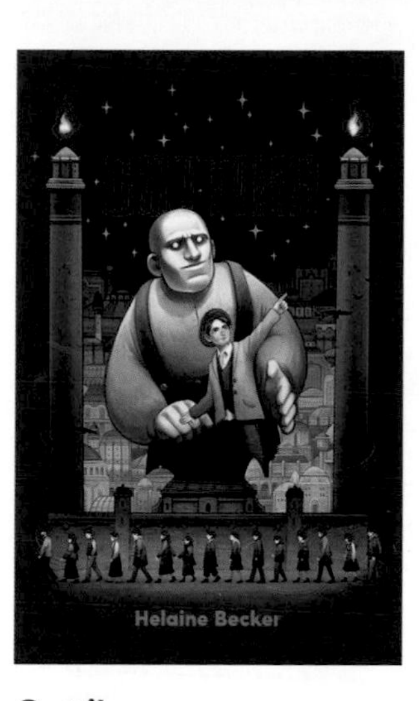

Gottika
Written by Helaine Becker
Illustrated by Vero Navarro

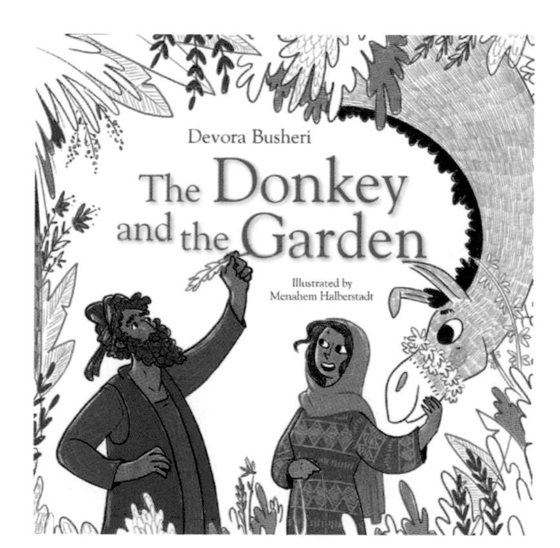

The Donkey and the Garden
Written by Devora Busheri
Illustrated by Menahem Halberstadt

The Wise Men of Chelm and the Foolish Carp
Written by Isaac Bashevis Singer
Illustrated by Viktoria Efremova

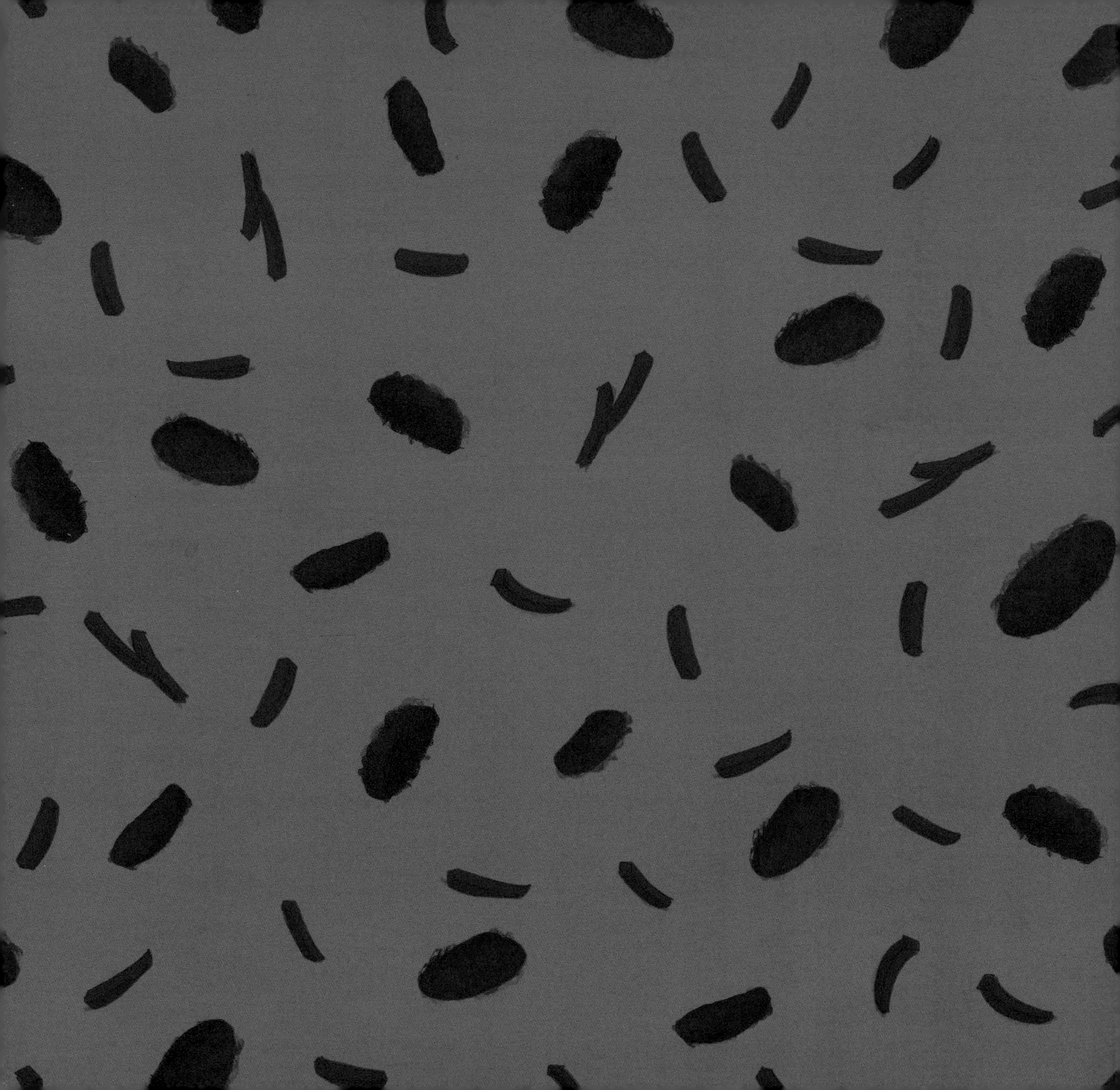